Lili

A Giant Panda
of Sichuan

Lili
A Giant Panda of Sichuan

ROBERT M. McCLUNG
Illustrated by IRENE BRADY

Morrow Junior Books · New York

1 2 3 4 5 6 7 8 9 10
Library of Congress Cataloging-in-Publication Data
McClung, Robert M.
Lili, a giant panda of Sichuan/Robert M. McClung ;
illustrated by Irene Brady.
p.   cm.
Bibliography: p.
Summary: Follows the first several years of a female giant panda
in the Chinese province of Sichuan and presents historical
commentary on human beings' relationship with pandas.
ISBN 0-688-06942-8. ISBN 0-688-06943-6 (lib. bdg.)
1. Giant panda—Juvenile literature.   [1. Giant panda.
2. Pandas.]   I. Brady, Irene, ill.   II. Title.
QL737.C214M339 1988
599.74'443—dc19
87-28271
CIP
AC

Contents

The Land of the Giant Panda

The heartland of Asia is the high Tibetan Plateau—the roof of the world, the remote crossroad for caravans from both East and West. To the north it is bounded by the rugged Tien Shan Range and the deserts of Mongolia. To the south loom the Himalayas, hundreds of jagged snow-capped peaks that stretch skyward higher than any other mountains in the world. The Vale of Kashmir—a wide lush valley surrounded by mountains—lies on its western rim; to the east is the vast and teeming land of China.

China's greatest river, the Chang Jiang, or Yangtze, rises in the Nan Shan Mountains of the Tibetan Plateau, then flows southward and eastward some 3,400 miles before emptying into the East China Sea. For much of the first third of its journey it winds through a barren, snow-covered wilderness, where it is joined by the white, foaming waters of many glacier-fed tributaries. It races downward through countless deep gorges, where turbulent waterfalls plunge over jagged cliffs and disappear in shimmering clouds of spray.

In China's Sichuan Province, the Min, Tuo, and Jialing Rivers join the Chang Jiang to form a mighty water highway that descends step by step from cold snowy highlands to the vast central plains of China. As the river flows, the East China Sea still lies some 2,500 miles to the east.

Sichuan is a land of bewildering contrasts, a region of towering mountain ranges and lowland valleys of almost tropical lushness—a region where wildlife from both the frozen north and the sun-loving south meet. The rare and beautiful snow leopard lives here, and the clouded and common leopards as well. Here the blue sheep, or bharal, clings to the high cliffs, and the takin—a relative of the musk-ox—forages in mountain meadows, together with strange goat-antelopes called goral and serow. Little tufted deer and musk deer lurk in the bamboo thickets, constantly alert to the dangers posed by foxes, wild red dogs, Himalayan black bears, and human hunters alike. Many colorful pheasants make Sichuan their home, as do Mandarin ducks and subtropical sunbirds.

The bamboo forests of Sichuan are also the home of the little red panda and the giant panda, an animal that was unknown to Western scientists until little more than a century ago. Today, the giant panda is known and loved throughout the world, even though it is one of the rarest animals on earth. Less than a thousand of them survive.

Lili
A Giant Panda
of Sichuan

The Birth of Lili

1

The setting sun bathed the snow-covered peaks to the west with a golden glow, but the nearby ridges were still snow-free in late October. Most of the birches and maples had already lost their leaves, but a few still flaunted thin mantles of red and yellow. The bamboo and rhododendrons were green as always. So were the pines, the hemlocks, and the spruces.

A little tufted deer ambled along the narrow game trail that threaded its way through an undergrowth of bamboo and sprawling shrubs. The tufted hair on its crown hid the short straight antlers, but the long canine teeth were visible as the tiny hoofed animal rooted through the debris on the forest floor, searching for seeds or green leaves to nibble on. Two snow pigeons whirred overhead, the white bands on their black tails flashing like signals in the fading light. Something had startled them.

The tufted deer stopped short, its big ears pricked forward, its nostrils twitching as it sniffed the air for possible danger. Its body tensed, ready for instant flight, as it heard the rustle of dried leaves in the undergrowth a short distance ahead. Something was coming. The tufted deer leaped into a thick stand of bamboo and disappeared.

A moment later, a big bearlike animal lumbered into view, its black-and-white body swaying from side to side as it ambled along the trail. It was a giant panda.

Ming's roly-poly body was mostly white, with her black markings making a striking contrast. Her legs were black, with the inky hue of her forelegs extending up-ward over each shoulder to form a black mantle across her back. A big circle of black fur surrounded each of her eyes, and her short rounded ears stuck up from her snowy head like fuzzy black powder puffs.

Ming was in a hurry, but she did not run. Instead, she advanced in a rapid, pigeon-toed walk as she headed toward her den. The smell of snow was in the air, and the time of birth of her first young was near.

After a few moments she left the twisting path through the bamboo and started to climb the steep slope to her left. Here the undercover of bamboo and shrubs was not so dense. A few towering firs and hemlocks reached skyward, and between these forest giants were scattered stands of birch and rhododendron. Ahead, a tiny nut-

hatch scuttled up and down a dead tree trunk, searching for insect pupae or eggs. Above it, a black-and-white woodpecker with a crimson nape hammered on a dead limb.

Ming paid no attention to the birds. She continued on toward the stub of a giant fir tree that had an opening in its base. Pausing at the teepeelike entrance to the stub, the panda peered in and sniffed noisily. Satisfied that her den was empty, she stepped inside. Turning round and round like a dog, she curled up on a bed of dried leaves with a low grunt. Soon she was asleep. Outside, snowflakes began to drift down as dusk faded into darkness.

It was nearly midnight before Ming stirred and then sat up. She blinked sleepily and peered outside, sniffling as she felt the wet snowflakes on her blunt nose. Retreating, she braced her back against the far wall of the den and waited. A few minutes later her first cub was born.

Bending down, Ming began to lick the tiny infant lying between her hind legs. When it was clean, she gently picked it up with her teeth and placed it on her breast. She continued to lick the baby from time to time, and soon it began to nurse.

Ming's first offspring was a female. No bigger than a chipmunk, Lili weighed only a quarter of a pound. Her body was pink and naked, except for a thin sprinkling

of white hair. Her tiny ears lay flat against her head, and her eyes were tightly closed.

Ming cuddled the helpless cub to her breast as she nursed and then curled up with Lili snug and warm between her legs. They both slept.

Late the next day, Ming ventured outside for a short

time to drink and eat. Before leaving the den, she gently picked Lili up in her jaws and carried the tiny infant with her. The snowfall had been light, but Ming's huge paws with their hairy brown soles left snowshoelike tracks behind her.

Stopping at a nearby brook, Ming laid the baby down on a bed of leaves while she drank long and deeply. When she had finished, she picked Lili up and crossed the stream on a moss-covered log. Heading for the nearest stand of bamboo, she ate hungrily, all the while holding Lili against her breast with one paw. Satisfied at last, she lumbered back to the shelter of the den.

Lili nursed many times each day and spent the rest of the time sleeping in her mother's paws or cuddled close to her warm, woolly body. The baby panda's belly was constantly round and full, and she grew and developed day by day. By the time she was a week old, Lili's fur coat had started to grow in, and black markings like her mother's were beginning to appear.

Ming was a good mother. Whenever she ventured out of the den, she carried Lili in her mouth or tucked against her breast with one encircling paw. Although she sometimes put the little cub down in a sheltered spot while she foraged in a nearby stand of bamboo, she seldom let Lili out of her sight. The baby was nearly a month old before Ming sometimes left her in the den while she ventured outside to feed.

Lili was as big as a half-grown kitten by this time and weighed two pounds—eight times as much as when she had been born. Her black-and-white coat was thick and woolly. Her eyes were beginning to open, and her black furry ears stood up. In many ways she looked just like her mother in miniature.

Close Encounters

2

In January, snow lay in thick drifts on the high ridges, and smoky plumes of fog and clouds floated over the frosty landscape every day. Lili was now two-and-a-half months old. As big and fat as a good-sized racoon, she weighed nine pounds and was starting to crawl about. Her eyes were fully open. Milk teeth were erupting in her gums. By springtime she would have a complete set of milk teeth, twenty-four in all. She was already beginning to nibble on tender leaves and stems of bamboo, but she still preferred her mother's milk.

Soon Lili began to take a definite interest in the life around her. She watched the winter birds—little rosy finches and black-crowned tits—as they flocked across the snowy slopes searching for seeds. Once, when Ming left her while she went off to feed, Lili saw a pair of musk deer browsing on winter buds and twigs as they walked past the den. They would not hurt her. Neither would the white-eyes—warblerlike birds with green-ish-yellow backs and chalky white breasts—that some-times flitted through the woodlands.

One morning while her mother was foraging, Lili played nearby. As she clambered up the slope of a fallen tree trunk, she heard soft chittering noises overhead. Looking up, she saw a band of a dozen or more animals swinging from branch to branch in the trees above her. They had long tails and thick coats of silky, golden fur. These were golden, or snub-nosed, monkeys.

One of them, with a baby clinging to her breast, swung low to get a better look at Lili. The little panda gazed back at the inquiring face. The mother monkey had a stubby, turned-up nose, and the bare skin around her velvety black eyes was a shining blue-green color.

The baby monkey stared at Lili and stretched one thin arm downward, as if it wanted to touch her. The little panda thrust her nose toward it and sniffed loudly. At that, the mother monkey bared her teeth and chit-tered nervously, then quickly swung back into the higher branches. A few moments later, the whole band trav-eled onward through the treetops. Golden monkeys live on the high, snowy slopes of central Asia, and eat the leaves of bamboo and other plants.

A few days later, Lili dozed at the entrance to the den while her mother foraged nearby. She was wak-ened by strange sounds unlike any she had heard be-

fore. Loud cries and shouts were coming from far down the slope, then strange chopping noises, repeated at regular intervals.

The noises were made by a band of men who were felling trees. They were woodcutters from the farms and the tiny village in the valley, far below.

Lili scrambled back into the den and lay silent and motionless, waiting for her mother to return. Something moved in the nearby bushes, and Lili watched as a boy wandered into view. He was the first human being she had ever seen.

Chang was the twelve-year-old son of one of the woodcutters. He had come with his father on the wood-cutting expedition—a rare treat, for it wasn't often he got this far from home. Now he was exploring the woods by himself, looking to see what he could see.

The boy stopped short when he spotted the black-and-white face of the little panda peering out of the den opening. Although he had lived in panda country all his life, Chang had never before seen a live one. His grandfather had told him stories of the *bei-shung*, or white bear, and he had seen the skin of a giant panda in the house of the village head man. Now, here was a living baby panda right in front of him.

Chang walked slowly toward Lili, talking softly as he advanced. He did not want to frighten the little panda. He just wanted a closer look at her. He knew that the government in far-off Beijing had passed laws protecting pandas. They were rare animals that lived only in a few remote areas of China. This part of Sichuan, where he lived, was one of them.

The boy came on slowly, step by step, making soft, friendly noises all the way. Finally he stopped and peered down at Lili. She gazed back, her eyes wide and staring.

To Chang, she appeared more curious than frightened. What a story he would have to tell his father and grandfather!

Chang's grandfather had been a noted hunter when he was a young man. The boy had grown up hearing the story of how his grandfather had helped an American lady capture a baby panda many, many years ago—before Chang's father had been born. The woman had taken the panda to far-off America, his grandfather said. She had named it Su Lin, and it was the first live giant panda ever seen outside of China. Now Chang could hardly wait to tell his grandfather about the baby panda that he had found.

Suddenly Ming burst out of a nearby clump of bamboo, grunting loudly and advancing as fast as she could go. She headed straight toward Chang, barking and chomping her teeth.

Startled, the boy jumped back. Then he turned and raced down the trail toward his father and the others.

Satisfied that Lili was safe, Ming halted her charge and went back to her young one. That evening the two pandas left their den and moved to a new home—a shallow cave under a rock ledge a half-mile farther up the slope.

Journey to the Lower Slopes

3

Winter began its retreat in late February. The snow started to melt on south-facing slopes and ice disappeared from the mountain streams. Soon the water was roaring down the gorges in foaming cascades, and buds began to swell on the trees. Spring was on its way.

Lili was four months old, and weighed almost sixteen pounds. She was active and playful. She still nursed, but was beginning to eat bamboo as well. Every day she was growing bigger and stronger.

By mid-April, new life was beginning to appear everywhere on the high slopes. The snow was gone, except in deep-shaded ravines. Grass and other shoots were pushing up through the matted layers of last fall's dead leaves. Crocus and anemone were among the first spring flowers in the woodlands, but it wasn't long before violets and irises carpeted the slopes as well. Buds were bursting on the birches and maples. Beneath them, rhododendrons began to flower. Some had clusters of pale pink blossoms. Others were red, or white, or orange.

Ming and Lili had roamed these high slopes all winter long, feeding on the leaves and stems of arrow bamboo. Now, as spring advanced, the two pandas began a slow, meandering journey down the ridges to the lower hills, where a different kind of bamboo—umbrella bamboo—grew in thick stands. This was the season when the umbrella bamboo sent up new growth. Its tender shoots are particularly juicy and fast growing, and Ming went down to feed on them nearly every spring.

Pandas usually roam the high slopes, from 8,000 to 12,000 feet above sea level, depending upon where they find the best stands of bamboo to eat. They seldom venture much lower except in springtime when some, such as Ming, go down to gorge on the tender shoots of umbrella bamboo. This species flourishes at lower altitudes, where the weather is milder, and sends up new growth at an earlier date than the arrow bamboo on the higher slopes.

For several days Ming and Lili wandered slowly downward, zigzagging back and forth as they traveled. Spring flowers were in bloom everywhere about them—violets and jack-in-the-pulpits, and big beds of trilliums with three-petaled blossoms of glowing white. In one tiny clearing they came upon an ancient pear tree in full bloom. A half-dozen little white-eyes and two gleaming red-and-blue sunbirds were flitting from branch to branch, feeding on the nectar in the white blossoms. A hen tragopan pheasant scurried in front of the two pandas, pursued by a gaudy male in bright orange and red courtship plumage.

The pandas came at last to a gentle hillside some 3,000 feet below their winter range. Here umbrella bamboo grew in thick stands, intermixed with birch and poplar. They passed some open fields as well— areas where woodcutters had felled big evergreen trees for lumber, or had cleared the land in preparation for planting crops. They saw several small huts or lean-tos where the men had lived while they were doing this work.

As the pandas walked along the edge of one clearing, they saw a small stone house with smoke rising from a hole in the roof. Far in the distance, they heard a dog barking. Ming quickly led Lili back into the forest. She did not want to run into either humans or dogs. She had had unpleasant encounters with both of them in the past.

Umbrella bamboo grew thick and lush nearly every-where they roamed. Day after day Ming stuffed herself with the tender, growing shoots. Sitting beside a thick clump of bamboo, she would break off a few shoots with her forepaws, then strip off the outer sheaths with her teeth. Pushing the shoots into her mouth one by one, she chewed and swallowed them. Her huge jaws were very powerful, and her rear grinding teeth, or molars, crunched easily through the green stems. Sometimes Ming would break off a larger woody stem. Before eating it, she would peel off the tough outer layers and discard them, leaving just the tender inner parts.

Each of Ming's forepaws had five fingers, all of them ending in a long claw. Each forepaw also had a leathery pad on it. This pad acted as a thumb for holding stalks of bamboo as Ming stripped and ate them. The pads were not true thumbs, like the opposable thumbs that human beings and monkeys use for grasping food and other objects. The panda's thumb is actually an elongated wrist bone covered with soft skin. However, it serves the same function that a real thumb does. It works as one side of a pair of pincers, of which the fingers are the other side.

By the end of May, Lili was almost completely weaned. Seven months old, she now ate bamboo as her mother did. She was increasingly active and playful. She rolled in the leaves of the forest floor and turned clumsy somersaults. She climbed up the slanting trunks of fallen trees and swatted at beetles that scurried ahead of her, or at a yellow butterfly that floated overhead. Sometimes, when Ming was sitting on her haunches, Lili would scramble up the slope of her mother's back and slide down.

One morning a hen tragopan crossed the path in front of the two pandas, followed by seven fluffy brown and yellow chicks. As Lili ambled over to investigate, the hen cried out a sharp warning to her young. They scattered in a twinkling and disappeared among the leaves of the forest floor.

That afternoon, Lili saw a little striped ground squirrel. Bouncing forward, she tried to catch it, but the little rodent whisked into its burrow with a sharp whistle of alarm.

Although pandas may eat mice or other small animals if they can catch them, almost all of their food is vegetable matter. They eat bulbs and roots and leaves of a number of different plants, but nine-tenths of their diet consists of the shoots, stems, and leaves of various kinds of bamboo. Bamboo is quite low in food value, however, and a panda has to eat great quantities of it in order to sustain itself. Ming, who weighed nearly 300 pounds, spent more than half of every twenty-four hours eating. She sometimes ate as much as forty pounds of bamboo in a day. The rough fibers passed through her digestive system so rapidly that they were only partly digested.

Between feedings, she rested or slept or traveled from one patch of bamboo to another. She was active both day and night. Her heaviest feeding periods, however, were during the early morning hours and in the late afternoon until dusk.

As the summer rainy season approached, Ming started the trip back to the high ridges. Until the next spring, she and Lili would feed on the arrow bamboo that grew there.

By October, when Lili was almost a year old, she

weighed seventy-five pounds. Fall colors had come once again to the high slopes—the gold and orange of birches and maples, the scarlet of dogwood and viburnum, the burnished browns of beeches and oaks. All of these colors were repeated in the plumage of a big male golden pheasant that strutted through the woodland early one frosty morning.

The next day, Ming and Lili were wakened by the sound of a dog barking in the distance; then they heard faint chopping sounds. Woodcutters had come up the mountainside to fell trees and gather wood, as they had the year before. Every year they were moving deeper into panda territory. Ming and Lili left their sleeping place and headed for a higher slope.

Two days later, the pandas once again heard a dog barking somewhere below them. But the sound came from much closer this time. In a few moments they spotted the dog—big and brown and shaggy, with a curled-up tail. It was coming up the narrow game trail, nose to the ground. The dog had picked up the panda's scent and was tracking them.

Ming and Lili started up the slope as fast as they could go, but the dog saw them and came rushing forward, yelping with excitement. Ming stopped and sent Lili scooting up into a maple tree. The young panda climbed up, hugging the trunk and humping upward like a caterpillar. Below, her mother turned to face the

dog, which was almost upon them. Ming bared her teeth and squealed as the dog charged toward her, then raised a forepaw to strike at her tormentor.

Coming face to face with the determined mother panda, the dog stopped abruptly and retreated to a safe distance. Still barking, it began to circle Ming, looking for an opening to attack. The panda turned with the dog, always facing it. After a moment the dog made a short rush toward her, but Ming was ready. She struck the dog with her clawed paw, sending it spinning backward. Yelping with pain, the dog backed away even farther.

Ming quickly turned and climbed up into the tree herself. In a moment she was on a limb beside the one where Lili sat. Made bold by the retreat of its opponent, the dog rushed forward, barking furiously as it gazed up at Ming and Lili. Safe in the high branches, the two pandas did not respond.

The dog remained under the tree for several hours, but the pandas did not stir. Dusk came, then night, and the pandas dozed on their lofty perches. When dawn came, the dog had vanished.

Land of Clouds
and Mist
4

In early November snow fell on the high ridges. Fog settled in the valleys and ravines, and rag-tag clouds swirled low over the ridges. Ming and Lili roamed their familiar haunts, eating their fill of bamboo and sleeping in any sheltered spot they could find. Sometimes they rested against the trunk of a fallen spruce or fir tree. Sometimes their bed was in a protected cleft under a ledge of rock. In December the weather turned bitterly cold, but their thick, woolly coats helped keep them warm. In such severe weather the two pandas often took shelter in the roomy den in the old fir stub, the place where Lili had been born.

Many other animals shared the winter slopes with them. Noisy jays flew over the steep hillsides, uttering their loud, piercing cries. Big black ravens sat in the treetops and cawed as the pandas passed beneath them. Partridges and snow pigeons often whirred up in startled flight ahead of them. Sometimes a little tufted deer or a musk deer bounded away at their approach.

One afternoon, after Ming and Lili had eaten their fill of bamboo, they settled down at the base of a high ledge of rock to sleep. A protective cover of rhododendron sheltered and hid them. It was nearly dusk when something wakened Lili.

Looking up, she saw a plump, short-tailed pheasant scratching in the snow and making soft clucking sounds as it searched for food. Its plumage was bright orange-red, deepening to crimson on its back. Its breast feathers had scalloped white edges, and the red feathers on its back were dotted with many tiny, black-encircled spots. Against the snow, the cock tragopan was a flashing target.

The big bird seemed to sense no danger, but Lili did. She had noticed a slight movement on the rock ledge some fifty feet behind the tragopan and about ten feet above it. Blinking, she focused her eyes on a huge cat that crouched there. The slight twitching of its long, plumelike tail had caught her eye. The big meat-eater's coat was a pale gray-blue, the color of wood smoke, and was marked with many scattered dark spots.

As the young panda watched, the snow leopard crept slowly forward, edging ever closer to the pheasant. At twenty-five feet it stopped and crouched, its hind quarters slightly raised and twitching back and forth as it

made ready to spring. At that moment Ming wakened with a wheezy snort. Startled, the pheasant took off with a whir of wings, just as the snow leopard sprang toward it. The big cat's leap was a split second too late.

Landing in the snow with a soft thud, the snow leopard whirled to face Ming and Lili, its tail whipping back and forth in frustration. The pandas had robbed it of its prey. Fangs bared in a snarl, ears laid back, the ghostly cat crouched once more, as though it might spring toward them. Then, with a low growl, it bounded back onto the ledge. In a moment it was gone.

When springtime came, the two pandas headed for the lower slopes once more. A year and a half old, Lili weighed 125 pounds, and was well able to take care of herself.

She lay at the base of a big maple tree one day while her mother foraged in a nearby stand of bamboo. Hearing crackling noises above her, she looked up. High on a limb of the maple sat a little furry animal with a bushy, ringed tail. Its coat was mostly bright rusty red, but it had a white face with black markings on the cheeks, and dark underparts.

As Lili stared at it, the little animal grasped a nearby branch of bamboo, using its forepaws as Lili did to seize and hold the branch. It chewed vigorously at the leaves. It was a red panda, the giant panda's closest relative.

The giant panda looks like a bear, while the red panda resembles a racoon. The giant and red pandas do not look alike, but they have many characteristics in common. Among these are the opposable "thumb," the mainly vegetarian diet, and the specialized structure of their jaws and teeth for crushing and chewing bamboo.

The red panda paid no attention to its big cousin on the ground beneath it. It continued to eat bamboo leaves

for a few moments, then stopped to lick its fur and groom itself. Soon another red panda that had been feeding nearby joined it. The two quickly slid to the ground and scampered away.

One morning in late May, Ming and Lili heard loud snuffling noises quickly followed by several loud bleats. A big male panda stalked out of a stand of bamboo and headed straight for them. Lili retreated behind her mother, but Ming did not seem to be alarmed.

As he approached, the male snorted loudly, then let out several loud yips. He wanted Ming for his mate. Ming looked at him for a moment, then ambled over to meet him. She was ready. The two pandas sniffed at one another, all the while squealing and chirping and making low murmuring noises deep in their throats. Then they turned and headed down the trail together. A mother panda usually leaves her yearling young when a prospective mate joins her. The young panda is well able to take care of itself by this time.

Lili gazed after the two adult pandas for a moment, then started to follow. Turning to face her, the big male barked sharply, then rejoined Ming. Lili hesitated for a moment, but soon began to follow them as before. The male panda turned once again. This time he growled at Lili and trotted a few steps toward her, chomping his teeth. Lili quickly retreated and climbed into a nearby tree. The male went back to Ming, who was waiting ahead, and the two of them disappeared into the underbrush. This time, Lili did not follow.

Ming had left Lili to go off with a mate. In the fall she would have young once again. From now on, Lili was on her own.

Territories and
Scent Posts

5

From that time on, Lili traveled alone. For the next several months, she stayed close to the old territory over which she and her mother had wandered, but that fall she moved onto a neighboring ridge. It supported many dense stands of bamboo, as well as forests of mixed evergreens and hardwoods. Some days Lili traveled as much as half a mile or more from the place where she had bedded down the night before, but often she was content to go no more than a few hundred yards.

All in all, the territory through which Lili wandered was nearly two miles long and a mile wide. Several other female pandas, including her mother, sometimes shared this territory with her. Lili encountered Ming several times that summer and fall, but after a casual sniffing of noses, the two would part company, each going her own way. The big male that had mated with

Ming occasionally wandered through the area too, but he no longer traveled with her.

Giant pandas usually live alone, except during the brief mating season, but they do not fight to protect their living space the way some animals do. Pandas living in neighboring areas wander freely over each others' territories. A female panda who is expecting young, or has newborn babies, however, usually claims a small part of the communal territory as her own, especially if her birthing den is in the area.

To mark the big territory over which they wander, adult pandas—especially males—leave their scent on tree trunks and rocks. One day Lili watched as a male panda stood on his forelegs and reared up against the trunk of a tall fir tree to smear the bark with scent from glands on either side of his tail. Finished, he turned, stood up on his hind legs, and stretching upward as far as he could, scratched the tree trunk with his sharp claws.

After he had gone, Lili approached the tree and examined it. She sniffed the male's distinctive, pungent scent and saw the long scratch marks high on the trunk. Such signals tell any panda coming by at a later date that this male had passed here. Adult female pandas also mark scent posts but not as often as males do. Many other animals—dogs and wolves, for example—also

leave their scents at certain places to signal to others of their kind that they have passed that spot.

One fall day, Lili wandered into a high mountain meadow where she encountered a band of animals unlike any she had seen before. The golden brown adults were as big as cows. They had humped backs and swollen noses. Their twisted horns curved out and forward, then back. These were takins, rare hoofed animals that live in Sichuan and other highlands in central Asia. Their closest living relatives are musk-oxen.

There were several old bulls in the takin band, together with a number of cows, yearlings, and smaller calves. Two of the biggest bulls were warily circling one another, stamping the ground with their front legs and snorting as each tried to intimidate the other. Watching from a screen of underbrush at the edge of the forest, Lili saw the two big animals charge one another and lock horns with a clattering thud. The two fighters pushed and shoved, each trying to make the other back up. The cows and young watched from a safe distance.

One of the calves wandered toward the stand of bamboo and rhododendron where Lili was watching. When the young takin saw her, it snorted with excitement. It had never seen a panda before. At the noise, the two bulls stopped their combat and stalked over to see what the calf had discovered. As they approached, Lili quickly climbed into a tree.

The two bull takins looked at her for a few moments, then wandered off into the meadow to graze. Neither they nor the other takins showed any further interest in her. But Lili did not come down from the tree until they finally wandered out of the meadow.

The Bamboo
Die-off
_____ 6

Lili was two years old that fall, and weighed about 175
pounds. She fed well that winter as she wandered through
her territory. Month after month she grew bigger and
stronger. Three or four years would pass, however, before she reached maturity and would be ready to accept
a mate.

The next spring, she headed down the slopes as usual
to fill up on umbrella shoots on the lower ridges. Now,
many of the bamboo stands she had first visited as a
youngster had been cut down and replaced by culti-
vated fields of maize, beans, or other crops. More of
the once-forested slopes had been cleared, as well. Every
year woodsmen were working higher and higher on
the mountainsides.

There was still enough bamboo in the area for Lili
and the other pandas to live on, however. But that

summer, when Lili was two-and-a-half years old, most of the arrow bamboo throughout a vast area around her territory flowered. Such an event happens in stands of bamboo only once or twice every hundred years. This flowering of the bamboo threatened disaster to the giant pandas that lived in the region.

Bamboo usually multiplies by sending out underground runners from its roots. These runners sprout shoots like those that Lili fed on every springtime. Stands of bamboo grow and spread in this way for many years without producing any flowers or seeds.

Perhaps once in a human lifetime, however, each kind of bamboo does flower and produce seeds. When the seeds ripen and fall to the ground, they sprout. After several years, the tiny plants become large enough to start a new stand. But after their flowering, the old plants that produced the seeds quickly wither and die. For a number of years after that, there may not be enough bamboo in the area to sustain animals such as pandas that depend upon it for food. Some of them may die of starvation.

That winter, after the die-off of the arrow bamboo, Lili wandered far and wide looking for healthy stands of bamboo to eat. She seldom found enough to satisfy her hunger. To keep healthy, pandas need to eat a great deal of bamboo every day. For lack of it, they slowly starve to death. Some of the giant pandas in the area did die that winter. The very old ones and the very young were the first victims.

Thin and weakened after her long, lean winter, Lili headed down the mountainside when springtime came, passing through many stands of withered and dead arrow bamboo. She hunted for the sprouting shoots of umbrella bamboo in the lower areas, but she found very little. Some of the old stands of umbrella bamboo had died. Others had been cut and cleared away by the farmers in the valley.

Passing along the edge of one of these clearings, Lili noted a slight movement among the dried leaves that covered the ground. A half-grown bamboo rat had poked its nose out of its burrow. Walking over, she saw many telltale signs of the furry rodents—small heaps of soil indicating entrances to burrows, as well as many bare stumps of bamboo harvested by the bamboo rats. Some of the burrow entrances were blocked with bamboo stems that the rats had tried to pull inside.

Lili began to dig into the honeycomb of burrows with her long, sharp claws. If she could catch a bamboo rat she would eat it. As she dug, several of the rats popped out of their nests and scurried away. Lili's claws finally exposed a nest cavity. There, on a bed of dried leaves, lay four baby bamboo rats, blind and naked. She quickly gulped them down.

The next day the young panda wandered even farther

down the slope, ever closer to the farmhouses in the valley. Ordinarily, Lili would never have ventured this close to human homes, but hunger had overcome her natural caution. That afternoon she found a few clumps of healthy bamboo near the edge of the woodland. She ate them, stalks and all, but there wasn't enough bamboo to satisfy her hunger.

Going on, she came to a low stone wall. Beyond it was a little shed, as well as several beehives made of sections of hollow tree trunks mounted on stone foundations. Lili sniffed the faint, sweet smell of honey in the air. She heard the humming of the bees as they came and went overhead, carrying pollen and nectar to the hives.

Scrambling over the low wall, Lili headed for the nearest hive and swept it to the ground with her paw. Angry swarms of bees began to buzz around her, but Lili ignored them. Her thick fur protected her from their stings. She began to gulp down the dripping honeycombs as fast as she could.

She heard a distant shout, then saw a man running up the slope toward her. Turning, Lili quickly retreated over the stone wall and into the thick brush above the clearing. Soon the farmer was left far behind.

Lili's hunger continued through the summer and early fall. During that time she came across the bodies of several pandas that had died. They were ragged and emaciated. Some of them had been ravaged by wild dogs, leopards, or other predators. These pandas had starved to death or had been so weakened that they were easy prey for hungry meat-eaters.

Chinese wildlife officials realized that many pandas were starving in the region where the bamboo had died. Supported by the government, they organized panda rescue teams. The groups were made up of wildlife biologists and farmers or woodcutters who were recruited in the area. These rescue teams were sent out to search for starving pandas and to supply them with food or, if they were too weak to survive in the wild, to try to capture them.

One October day, a rescue team of three men—their leader a wildlife biologist—stumbled upon Lili as she dozed, curled up at the base of a big beech tree. The men approached cautiously, but Lili woke up as they neared her. She gazed at them with bleary eyes.

The men immediately stopped, waiting to see what the panda would do. The youngest member of the team was Chang. He was now almost sixteen years old. He still remembered how excited he had been when he had seen the little panda cub three years before. That recollection had prompted him to volunteer for one of the panda rescue teams.

Chang edged closer to Lili. He wondered whether

she might be the same panda, now grown up. She was in the same general area and looked like a young animal. It was possible, he told himself. Stopping a few feet from her, he opened a bag he was carrying and took out several flat cakes made of cornmeal and cooked rice, mixed with honey and water. Laying these down in front of the panda, he backed off a short distance. Then he and the others waited to see what she would do.

Lili sniffed loudly, smelling the welcome odor of cornmeal and honey. Getting up, she cautiously approached the food and began to eat. She did not stop until every scrap was gone. Then she looked up for more. The only food the men had left was their own lunches—rice and chicken. Chang offered his meal to the hungry panda, and after a moment the other two followed suit. Lili quickly gulped it down. Then she turned and began to walk up the slope. Chang and the others gazed after her with smiles on their faces. They knew that they had helped at least one panda that day.

The headquarters of the rescue team was in an abandoned hut that had been used by woodcutters in years past. The hut was some distance down the slope, near the center of the vast area where the arrow bamboo die-off had occurred. Every day the men roamed the slopes looking for hungry pandas and putting out food in regular locations for those they found. The team also built several big log traps and baited them with food. They hoped to capture some of the starving pandas and release them in distant areas where there was plenty of bamboo.

One day, as Lili headed for the spot where the men had been leaving food for her, she saw what looked like a big square box made of logs in a small clearing just ahead. It was about seven feet long and three feet wide and high. One end of the box was open, with a heavy wooden panel looming above the opening.

Lili peered suspiciously at the strange structure. Then, smelling food, she approached the big log box and peered inside. The box was empty, except for a small heap of food near the back. She sniffed. It was meat of some kind. Unable to resist the smell, Lili entered the box and began to eat the goat meat and cornmeal mush laid out for her. As she picked up the meat, she triggered the trap, and the wooden door slammed down behind her. She was caught in the big box.

Lili turned around in her cramped prison, trying to find a way out. She clawed at the logs and chewed at them, but they would not budge. Finally she accepted that she was trapped. She lay down, peered out through a narrow space between two logs, and waited.

After several hours, she heard voices, then saw three men approaching. They were Chang and the two other men of the rescue team—the men who had been put-

ting food out for her. The men exclaimed excitedly when they realized that the trap door had been tripped. Something was inside. Peering between the logs, they saw Lili. She huffed at them, then sniffed loudly.

Chang and the others talked rapidly to one another, deciding what they would do. After a few moments the two older men headed down the slope toward the head-quarters hut as fast as they could go. They would bring back a cage they had there. Chang stayed behind to look after the panda.

When the other two had gone, Chang came up beside the trap cage and talked to Lili in a low, friendly voice. He shoved several rice cakes into the trap through a space between two logs, and watched as she sniffed at them, and then gulped them down. She did not seem to be frightened. Was it because she was too weak with hunger? Chang asked himself. Or was she used to seeing him by now?

After a couple of hours, the other two members of the rescue team returned, bringing with them a big, lightweight cage made of aluminum and wire. A third man came with them, too, as four would be needed to carry the cage when the panda was in it. Working quickly, they placed the cage next to the trap, and opened its sliding metal door. Next, they pulled up the big wooden door of the log trap. The way was clear for Lili to leave the trap and go into the cage.

Lili peered out of the open end of her log prison. She blinked, then slowly walked into the cage. The men quickly closed the door behind her and locked it.

Picking up the cage, two men on either side, they started down the rough, narrow path. The cage jounced up and down with every step. Lili lay down and looked out between the bars while the men passed the head-quarters hut, trotted across an open clearing, and finally came to a narrow, winding dirt road. There, a small pickup truck was waiting.

The four men lifted the cage with Lili in it onto the open bed of the truck. Then Chang got into the cab, along with the leader of the rescue team, the wildlife biologist. Starting the engine, the biologist drove off, following the winding road that had been built into the slope. They passed through the little village in the valley, then drove onward for nearly fifteen miles through groves of dead bamboo. For most of the time, they were within sight of a mountain stream.

At last they entered a small valley where stands of living bamboo grew along either side of the road. On they went for several more miles, through areas where the bamboo was fresh and green and flourishing. The team leader finally stopped the truck in a small clearing beside the stream. He and Chang got out of the cab. Between them, they picked up Lili's cage and put it on the ground.

Lili was weak and thin, as they well knew. But she was still able to walk about. She could find plenty of food in this area and grow strong and healthy once again. Chang and the biologist opened the cage door. Then they backed off and waited to see what the panda would do.

Lili stepped cautiously out of the cage. She peered about and sniffed, then walked over to the stream and drank. After a few moments she wandered over to the nearest stand of bamboo and began to eat.

Chang and the team leader watched approvingly. They smiled at one another. The panda should do all right in this area. They continued to watch Lili for another hour. Finally she wandered up the slope and disappeared into the forest. Then the two men climbed into the truck and drove off. Chang knew that he would come back whenever he could to try to locate this panda and check on her again.

Mating Time _____7

Lili found plenty to eat in the new area. Her lean body slowly filled out, and within months her coat became thick and healthy once again.

By late winter of her sixth year she weighed nearly 300 pounds. She was a full-grown adult panda, as big as she ever would be. Her winter coat was thick and heavy, the white fur clean and lustrous against her black markings.

Snow still lay in deep drifts through the shaded ravines in late February, but under the warm March sun it soon began to melt on many exposed slopes.

When Lili walked along a barren hillside still covered with snow, the black markings of her coat stood out like moving spots of ink. But when she was in the woods, winding her way between the dark tree trunks and through stands of bamboo or rhododendron, she was almost invisible. Here, her black-and-white pattern

blended into the shifting light and shadows of the wooded background. When she was sleeping or dozing against a log, few humans or animals that passed nearby would notice her.

Soon the snow disappeared entirely. Spring flowers began to appear on the lower slopes where Lili was feeding on shoots of new bamboo. One sunny morning in April, two little yellow butterflies skittered past her, one chasing the other. Finches called to one another in the nearby trees, and a pair of crows cawed from their nest high in a spruce. Spring was a time for courtship and mating.

A cock golden pheasant with long, sweeping tail feathers strutted past, displaying his bright plumage before a dusky brown hen. His crest gleamed like burnished gold, and from time to time he spread his bright orange ruff like a fan, each flaming feather tipped with blue-black. The cock's trim body glittered with iridescent reds, blues, greens, and yellows. The hen pheasant, however, seemed unimpressed. She wandered back and forth, pecking idly at sprouting shoots.

Lili watched the two pheasants while she ate. The hen finally slipped into the underbrush and the cock followed. Soon Lili wandered on, too. She was feeling a strange restlessness, something she had never yet experienced. Passing a scent tree marked by other pandas before her, she paused to sniff, then reared up and rubbed her own scent on the signpost. Afterward, facing the tree, she scratched at its ragged bark for a moment before going on.

With the sun high overhead, she lay down at the base of a fallen hemlock to sleep. Sunshine, sifting through the branches, cast flickering patterns of light and darkness all about her. A pair of squirrels chased one another around the trunk of the tree, and a blue rock thrush perched on a branch and sang to a nearby female.

Lili was wakened by a snuffling noise, followed by several shrill barks. She got up, her dark eyes blinking, the catlike slits of her pupils narrowing in the bright sunshine. She noticed movement in the underbrush, not far from her; in a moment a big male panda appeared. He was coming toward her. This courting male had followed Lili's wandering trail through the forest.

The male bleated when he caught sight of Lili and approached eagerly. Lili clacked her jaws together nervously, her teeth clicking against one another in a rapid tattoo. She was not yet ready to mate. She yipped at the male, warning him to keep his distance. Then she turned and headed into the shadows of the forest. The male followed.

When he got too close, Lili turned and faced him once again, teeth clicking. The male backed off and Lili lumbered on. She was not frightened of the other panda.

He meant her no harm. But she wasn't yet ready to mate with him, either.

The male was persistent. From time to time, as he followed, he left his scent on a tree trunk, then scratched the bark with his claws. In this fashion he trailed behind Lili all day. That night she climbed high into a tall fir tree and slept there. The big male waited below.

On the morning of the third day, Lili at last allowed the male to approach her. He grunted softly as she nosed him. Lili turned to move on, then looked back, encouraging the male to come with her. Soon they were feeding together. That afternoon they mated.

The big male panda remained with Lili for two more days, and they mated a number of times. Then he wandered off and Lili took up her solitary life as before—with one difference. Now she carried new life within her.

In October, five months after she had mated, Lili gave birth to two cubs—a male and a female—in a sheltered rock cave. She had dragged leaves and small branches into the cave to form a bed, and the den was snug and secure. Both of the babies were healthy and vigorous. As soon as they were born, Lili licked the two young ones clean. Then she nursed them.

When she left the den to forage the next day, she took the male cub, the larger of the two babies, with her, carrying him in her mouth. The little female was left behind, for Lili could not carry both infants with her as she traveled. This arrangement continued for the next few days.

One morning, about two weeks later, she carried the young male with her, clasping him to her breast with her forepaw, when she left the den to forage. Before feeding, she laid him carefully on the ground beside

her. When her hunger was satisfied, she picked the baby up and returned to the den.

As she approached it, she heard a low snarl. Hurrying ahead as fast as she could go, she was just in time to see a big spotted leopard come out of the cave with the other baby panda in its jaws. Spotting Lili, the leopard growled threateningly, deep in its throat. Then it bounded away and disappeared in the forest.

Still clutching her one remaining young, Lili started to lumber after the leopard, but soon stopped. The big cat could travel much faster than she could. There was no possibility of rescuing her other baby. Turning, she headed up the hillside away from the birthing den. She needed to find a new den for herself and the remaining youngster.

Late that afternoon she bedded down in a giant hollow log, not far from a mountain stream. The new den was almost a mile away from the old one in the rock cave. She licked the whimpering baby and held it as it nursed.

The Panda
Reserve

8

Lili's surviving youngster stayed with her until his second spring, when Lili took a mate once again. When she did, the yearling panda wandered off on his own, just as Lili had left her mother a half dozen years before.

Pandas may live for twenty-five years or more and, as the years passed, Lili gave birth to one or two young every second or third year. She had twins more often than not but was never successful in raising both of them. She could not carry both infants with her when she left her den. One of them was always left behind.

One winter, a pack of wild dogs, or dholes, found one of the babies in the den and killed it. Two years after that, a yellow-throated marten—a big member of the weasel family—carried off another of Lili's offspring. Just a week later, her surviving young one was carried away by a red fox which had trailed her and had seen where she placed the little panda while she

58

foraged. It had burst out of the underbrush, snatched up the young one in its jaws, and bounded away before Lili could come to the baby's rescue.

Two-and-a-half years after the fox had stolen her young, Lili roamed the familiar lower hillsides one May morning, feeding on umbrella bamboo. At her side was her latest offspring—Pan, a lively, six-month-old male.

These slopes over which Lili roamed were now within the boundaries of a new wildlife reserve which the Chinese government had established to protect giant pandas and other animals. The Chinese were very proud of their pandas and realized how few of them survived. They wanted to protect and help them as much as possible.

A little musk deer darted across the path in front of the two pandas, and a laughing thrush whistled from a nearby birch tree. Lili and Pan approached a sunny ledge. Her belly full of bamboo, Lili lay back against the warm rock to doze. The baby nestled against her and they both slept.

It was late afternoon when Lili wakened, feeling the little panda on her back. Pan had wakened before her and was playing. Sliding down his mother's furry side, he rolled in the grass, then climbed up to try the slide once again.

Gently shoving her offspring away, Lili got up and started down the narrow trail toward the next stand of bamboo. She was hungry and wanted another meal before dark. Pan followed at her side. Lili kept a close watch on the youngster. He was still too small and defenseless to be out of her sight for long. When the little one waddled ahead, chasing after a white butterfly, Lili followed.

Suddenly a bent sapling a short distance ahead snapped

upright with a sharp humming sound. Pan gave a bleat of pain and surprise as his left hind leg was hoisted into the air, caught tight by a loop of wire attached to the sapling. The little panda had stepped into a snare that poachers had set for musk deer. These little animals are valued for the musk pod on their belly, which is used in making perfume. The round wire noose had been placed in the center of the trail and covered with dried leaves. When Lili's baby stepped into the noose, he had triggered the trap, causing the sapling to spring up.

The youngster squalled loudly as he pulled at the wire, struggling to be free. But Pan's struggles only made the wire squeeze even tighter into the flesh of his leg. The little panda turned and bit at the wire, trying to free himself; then he whimpered as Lili hurried to him.

When Lili discovered the wire holding the baby's leg, she seized it in her teeth and tried to break it, but without success. The wire was too strong. Finally the little panda lay back panting. He was exhausted. Lili sat down beside him and he crept as close to her as he could. Pan whimpered, then nestled between her legs and began to nurse. By the time he had finished, dusk had fallen.

The full moon rose over the slopes, casting pale shadows through the bamboo and rhododendron. Lili dozed, and so did her baby, exhausted by his struggles. It was almost midnight, with the moon high overhead, when something wakened Lili.

A pale spotted creature—a big cat—was circling her and the young panda, just a few feet away. The leopard had spotted the two of them while it was hunting. It had no interest in challenging Lili. She was too big. It would like to take the little panda, however. Now it circled, tail twitching, watching and waiting for the opportunity to dash in and seize Pan.

Lili swung to face the big cat as it circled about them. The young panda huddled between her legs. Lili barked at the leopard and made a short lunge toward it, brave in defense of her young. The big meat-eater backed away a few steps, its ears laid back, its long canine teeth bared in a snarl. It was not willing to take on the embattled mother panda face to face, however.

The standoff continued for many minutes—the leopard circling, Lili turning to face it, waiting for it to attack. At length the big cat retreated. It could find easier prey elsewhere.

Lili watched it disappear into the forest. The youngster was quiet once again, secure against his mother's plump side. Lili remained awake through the remaining hours of the night, alert and watchful. The moon sank and set; finally dawn began to lighten the eastern sky.

Chang walked up the forest trail that morning to check a panda trap located farther up the slope. He was twenty-four years old now, a member of the staff of the panda reserve that the government had established in this area.

Far ahead, near the top of the ridge, he heard crows calling. Then, as he hurried onward, he heard muffled barks and bleats. Finally he spotted Lili. Beside her was her young one, with its hind leg caught in a wire noose. The little panda was struggling to free itself.

Chang knew at once what had happened. Like several other unfortunate pandas, this little one had blundered into a snare. Chang had found a half-grown panda dead in a similar trap several months before. Traps of any kind were illegal in the wildlife reserve, but poachers didn't care about the law.

Chang advanced cautiously toward the two pandas. He must release the young one as quickly as possible. But how—with the big panda standing guard?

Lili watched intently as the young man came closer and closer; then she barked a warning. Chang stopped immediately and began to talk to her, his voice quiet, his words calm and soothing.

"Don't worry, old one," he told her. "I won't hurt your baby. All I want to do is help it—free it. That's what you want, too."

He took a slow step forward, then another, talking all the while. Lili responded to the calm, friendly tone. She had heard it before, and no harm had come to her. She snorted uneasily, then backed slowly away as Chang approached even closer. The little panda was quiet as it saw the man coming toward it.

Chang never took his eyes off Lili as he advanced, step by step. The mother panda was no more than thirty feet away as he squatted beside her baby. Chang knew that he was taking a risk. He didn't know what he would do if the big panda decided to charge him.

Kneeling beside Pan, he worked swiftly to loosen the

wire loop from around his leg. Chang stroked the little panda's soft woolly fur as he worked at the noose. Pan blinked, but did not struggle. Lili did not rush him, either.

At last the youngster's leg was free. Chang patted him gently, then backed away to a safe distance.

For a few moments, Pan did not realize that he was free. When he did, he started running toward his mother. In a moment he was by her side. Chang was pleased to see that the young one barely limped. He had released it in time, before the circulation in its leg had been completely cut off. This little panda would be all right.

Meeting her offspring, Lili bent to lick his face. She looked toward Chang for a long moment, then turned and walked into a stand of bamboo. The young one followed. Chang watched as they disappeared into the forest.

The Giant Panda

Legendary Past, Endangered Present, Uncertain Future

The Chinese have known for thousands of years that a large bearlike animal with peculiar black-and-white markings roamed the high mountain areas of their country that spilled down from the Tibetan highlands. Some called this strange beast *bei-shung* or *pei-hsiung*, meaning "white bear." Others called it *hui-hsiung*, or "spectacled bear." Today, many Chinese know the animal as *daxiong mao*, "great bear-cat."

To Americans, it is the giant panda. The species was unknown to Western scientists until little more than a century ago.

The Giant Panda in History

In 1869, Abbé Armand David, a French missionary-naturalist, secured several specimens of the giant panda

while on an exploring and collecting trip through the ancient kingdom of Muping, in the highlands of western China.

"My Christian hunters return today after a ten-day absence," Armand David recorded in his diary for March 23. "They bring me a young white bear, which they took alive but unfortunately killed so it could be carried more easily." The Frenchman viewed this prize as a new species of bear, ". . . very remarkable not only because of its color, but also for its paws, which are hairy underneath, and for other characters."

Père David wasted no time in sending a written description of the species to his friend, Professor Alphonse Milne-Edwards, who was on the staff of the Paris Museum of Natural History. He called his find *Ursus melanoleucus,* the "black-and-white bear." A few days after this, the missionary-naturalist's hunters brought him an adult panda. The skins and skulls of the two specimens were subsequently sent to Milne-Edwards.

For nearly sixty years afterward, no other specimens of the giant panda were secured for science, and practically nothing new was added to the knowledge of the mysterious animal. It remained an almost unknown and legendary beast.

In the late 1920s and the early 1930s, however, several American scientific expeditions were mounted with the primary objective of collecting giant pandas. In 1928,

Theodore and Kermit Roosevelt, sons of former President Theodore Roosevelt, led an expedition backed by the Chicago Field Museum into panda country. They shot one adult male panda which can be seen in the museum today. Collecting for the same museum several years later, a British hunter, Floyd Tangier Smith, purchased two specimens from local hunters in Sichuan.

In 1931 the Philadelphia Academy of Science sponsored a second expedition. Ernest Schaeffer, a young naturalist with the group, shot a male panda. Three years after that, a third expedition sponsored by the American Museum of Natural History in New York, and led by Dean Sage, bagged another giant panda. Three skins were also purchased from native hunters.

Thus, by 1934, three museums in America had secured specimens of the giant panda. Scientists could study these to learn more about the anatomy and physical characteristics of the species. Very little was as yet known about pandas in the wild, however—their habits, characteristics, and requirements.

The First Giant Panda in Captivity

It was about this time that William Harkness, a wealthy New Yorker who was an enthusiastic naturalist-adventurer and also a devotee of the New York Zoo-

logical Society, decided to go to China and collect a living giant panda for the Bronx Zoo. Everyone agreed that such an undertaking, if successful, would be one of the great events of zoo history.

When he disembarked at Shanghai, Harkness began to prepare for his trek into the interior with the help and advice of Floyd Tangier Smith, who had traveled in panda country and had already secured several panda skins for the Chicago Field Museum. The two men experienced one obstacle after another, however, and the expedition was delayed. In February, 1936, Harkness died unexpectedly in Shanghai.

Before leaving for China in 1934, Harkness had married a chic New York dress designer. His new wife, however, did not accompany him on the panda expedition. He evidently thought that a trip into the rugged wilderness of western China would be much too difficult for a city-bred woman.

When Ruth Harkness learned of her husband's death, she at once determined to sail for China, pick up the loose ends of the expedition, and search for a giant panda herself. She realized that she knew little about animals, nothing about organizing an expedition, and practically nothing about China. But she could learn.

Arriving in Shanghai in July, 1936, Ruth Harkness hired a wiry Chinese youth, Quentin Young, as her

assistant. Quentin, who spoke English as well as Chinese, was a younger brother of Jack Young, who had accompanied the Roosevelts on their expedition eight years before. Together, Ruth Harkness and Quentin Young gathered the necessary equipment and planned the details of the proposed expedition. The journey would include a trip of 1,500 miles up the Chang Jiang, or Yangtze River to Chongqing (Chunking), then an overland trip of some 300 miles to Chengdu, the capital of Sichuan Province. This would be their push-off point for a rugged trip by foot to the remote high country where the giant pandas roamed.

Reaching Chengdu in mid-October, they immediately started toward the snow-covered mountains that rose, tier on tier, to the west. They crossed the Min River on a swaying bamboo bridge, then climbed up and over many rugged hills on narrow paths. On October 30 they arrived at Tsaopo, a tiny village of cobbled streets and primitive stone houses. They were at the edge of panda country at last.

In this "land of clouds and mist" they quickly established a base camp which Ruth Harkness used as her headquarters, while Quentin Young went a few miles farther west to set up another temporary camp. The search for pandas began in earnest, with the help of native hunters and trappers.

On November 9, Ruth Harkness followed Quentin Young as he led the way to his advance camp. They heard a shout from one of their hunters ahead of them, then the sound of a gun being fired. Hastening on through the snow, they came to a huge, rotting tree. "From the old dead tree," Ruth wrote, "came the sound of a baby's whimper." Quentin ran forward to investigate. In a moment he headed back toward her, holding something in his arms. "There in the palms of his hands was a squirming baby *bei-shung.*"

They learned from their hunter that he had seen an adult panda and had shot at it, but it had escaped. The little one, which Ruth cuddled in her arms, was presumably its baby. The little panda was christened Su Lin—"a little bit of something very cute." In February, 1937, it ended up not at the Bronx Zoo in New York but at the Chicago Brookfield Zoo.

How Ruth Harkness found the baby panda and brought it back to the United States after surmounting many difficulties make fascinating reading, as related in her book, *The Lady and the Panda,* which was published the next year.

First thought to be a female, Su Lin turned out on later examination to be a male. As the first giant panda ever exhibited outside its native land, Su Lin proved a stellar attraction with the zoo public and press alike.

———————

Other Zoo Pandas

Flushed by her success, Ruth Harkness returned to China and brought back a second young panda for the Brookfield Zoo in February, 1938. The flow of giant pandas to the world's great zoos had begun. The Bronx Zoo got its first specimen in June of that year. In December, Floyd Tangier Smith sailed from Shanghai with no less than *six* giant pandas that had been captured by his native trappers. One died en route to Europe, but five of them eventually arrived at the London Zoo.

The Bronx Zoo got its second panda in May, 1939. Two more arrived there in December, 1941, shortly after the outbreak of the Pacific war with Japan.

In every Western zoo lucky enough to have them, giant pandas attracted great crowds, for the zoo public found the cuddly appearance and playful antics of these exotic black-and-white teddy bears irresistible.

During World War II the flow of pandas out of China ceased until the coming of peace in August, 1945. After that, the panda exodus began again. By the end of the next year, there were a total of fourteen pandas in Western zoos. Since that time, China has sent giant pandas to zoos in London, Moscow, Washington, D.C., New York, Tokyo, Paris, Mexico City, Madrid, and Pyong Yang. Many have been exhibited in Chinese zoos as well.

Through observations and study of these pandas, a great deal has been learned about panda care and requirements in captivity. It was not until the late 1970s, however, when serious field studies of the species were undertaken, that Chinese and Western scientists began to learn more about the habits and requirements of giant pandas in the wild.

The Giant Panda Today

When Professor Milne-Edwards examined the remains of the two giant pandas that Père David had sent him in 1869, he quickly realized that although the missionary-naturalist considered the giant panda a bear, the species had some unique physical characteristics quite different from those of typical bears. He placed the giant panda in a new genus, *Ailuripoda*, or "panda-foot." Today the species is known scientifically as *Ailuripoda melanoleuca*, the "black-and-white panda-foot."

Ever since its discovery by Western scientists, the proper place in the classification system of both the giant panda and its little relative, the red panda, has been argued by mammalogists. Some say the two are most closely allied to the bears, while others opt for the racoon family. The consensus now seems to be that the two pandas should be placed in a separate family of their own, the *Ailuridae*, but that they are probably most closely allied to the bears.

The location of fossil remains indicate that the giant panda once ranged over much of western China, as well as over portions of neighboring Tibet and western Burma. Today, that range has shrunk to a few scattered pockets of rugged mountain territory, most of them in Sichuan, where the panda still finds suitable habitat and the stands of bamboo that it needs.

During the widespread bamboo die-offs in northern Sichuan, from 1974 to 1977, the first extensive survey of giant panda numbers and distribution was undertaken by the Chinese government, along with efforts to rescue and relocate starving pandas. This first panda census indicated that no more than 1,100 giant pandas survived in the wild.

In recent years the People's Republic of China has created many reserves to protect its wildlife. Twelve of these have been set aside primarily for the protection of the giant pandas that live in them. An estimated sixty percent of the total world population of pandas live in these reserves.

The Wolong Reserve

The Wolong Reserve, nearly 800 square miles of rugged

U.S.S.R.

Tibetan Plateau

Himalayas

NEPAL

BHUTAN

BANGLADESH

INDIA

BURMA

Present Giant
Panda Range

Panda Reserves

Bay of Bengal

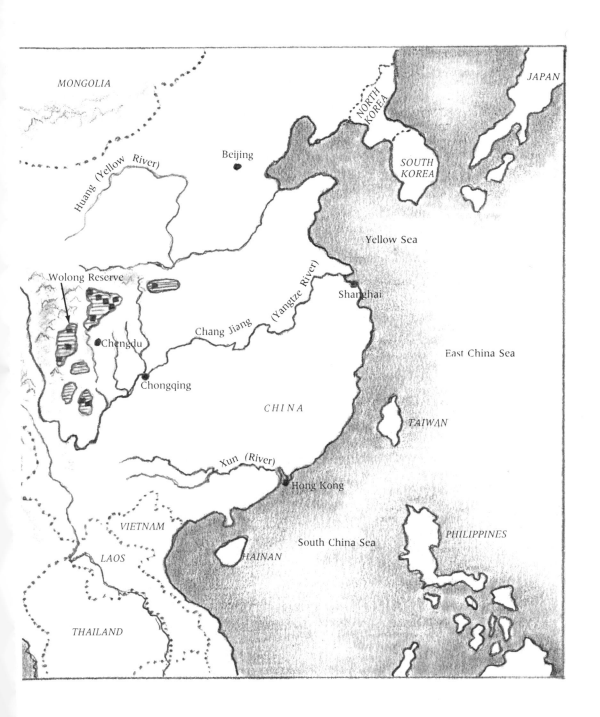

MONGOLIA

Huang (Yellow River)

Beijing

NORTH KOREA

SOUTH KOREA

JAPAN

Yellow Sea

Wolong Reserve

Chang Jiang

(Yangtze River)

Shanghai

Chengdu

East China Sea

Chongqing

CHINA

TAIWAN

Xun (River)

Hong Kong

VIETNAM

LAOS

HAINAN

South China Sea

PHILIPPINES

THAILAND

forested slopes and valleys, situated in the Qionglai Mountains some eighty miles northwest of Chengdu, is probably the most important panda reserve.

It was at Wolong, in 1980, that a team of scientists, headed by Hu Jinchu, China's leading panda expert, and George Schaller, Director of Wildlife Conservation International, of the New York Zoological Society, launched an ambitious five-year program of giant panda research. This program was sponsored jointly by China and the World Wildlife Fund.

During the course of the research, a number of Wolong's pandas were trapped and outfitted with radio collars so that their daily and seasonal movements and activities could be followed and charted. Teams of scientists are still tracking these pandas in this manner today, and studying them in the wild.

A giant panda conservation, research, and breeding station was completed at Wolong in 1984; it includes laboratories, an animal hospital, a nursery for baby pandas, and living quarters for the scientists and staff. Wolong's first birth of a panda in captivity occurred at the station in 1986; at present, nearly a dozen captive pandas are housed there.

The Chinese also have pandas in zoos in Beijing, Shanghai, Chengdu, and a number of other cities. Between 1963 and 1985, nearly fifty litters have been born to these zoo pandas. Some of these births have been the result of artificial insemination; the first was in the Beijing Zoo in 1978. Continued success with zoo breeding programs may eventually result in the release of some captive-bred pandas to the wild. Outside of China, panda births have occurred at the Chapultepec Zoo in Mexico City, Tokyo's Ueno Zoo, the Madrid Zoo, and the National Zoo in Washington, D.C.

An Uncertain Future

In spite of the knowledge gained from field studies and the encouraging success with captive breeding programs, the endangered giant panda faces a very uncertain future.

A new panda census completed in the autumn of 1986 indicates a decline in wild panda numbers to between 600 and 700. These are fragmented into about thirty-five small, scattered "island" populations of less than twenty individuals—each population separated from others by impassable barriers such as rivers, high, steep ridges, or areas of clear-cut forest. The decline is evidently due to steady human encroachment, bad forestry practices, and periodic bamboo die-offs. If the decline continues, the giant panda could be extinct in the wild by the early years of the twenty-first century.

Alarmed by the steady decline of the panda population, the World Wildlife Fund declared a "panda emergency" in March, 1987, and launched a worldwide campaign to raise funds to help save the species. A joint World Wildlife Fund–Chinese Ministry of Forestry team has drafted a plan to preserve the species by protecting existing stands of bamboo, by establishing pathways with new plantings of bamboo that will connect isolated panda populations, and by improving the captive breeding program. Efforts will also be made to stop the human invasion of panda habitat as much as possible—even to the relocation of farm families and villages where necessary.

The giant panda is the symbol of the World Wildlife Fund, an organization dedicated to the saving and protecting of endangered wildlife everywhere. Pandas are favorites with millions of people all over the world. They want the panda to survive, not only in captivity but also—even more important—in its natural wilderness home.

"The panda is . . . more than an animal, more than mere muscle, bone, and skin," George Schaller has observed. "It is a symbol of China's conservation effort and of the world's."

For Further Reading

Books marked with an asterisk were written for young readers. The others are aimed primarily at adult readers, but contain a great deal of information and many illustrations that should be of interest to young readers as well.

Fox, Helen M. (Translator and editor). *Abbé David's Diary*. Cambridge: Harvard University Press, 1949. Account of the French missionary-naturalist's exploration of panda country in 1869.

Harkness, Ruth. *The Lady and the Panda*. New York: Carrick and Evans, Inc., 1938. How the author found and brought to America the first baby panda ever seen in the Western world.

*Jin Xuqi and Kappeler, Markus. *The Giant Panda*

(translated by Noel Simon). New York: G. P. Putnam's Sons, 1986. Short account of the giant panda's life, habits, and requirements, illustrated with many outstanding color photographs.

MORRIS, RAMONA and DESMOND. *Men and Pandas.* New York: McGraw-Hill Book Company, 1966. Interesting and well-researched account of pandas in the wild, in zoos, and throughout history.

————. (Revised by Jonathan Barzdo). *The Giant Panda.* London: Kogan Page Ltd., 1981. A revised, retitled, and updated version of the Morrises' 1966 book.

PERRY, RICHARD. *The World of the Giant Panda.* New York: Taplinger Publishing Co., 1969. A popular account of the giant panda in history and in the wild.

*RAU, MARGARET. *The Giant Panda at Home.* New York: Alfred A. Knopf, 1977. An account of a year in the life of wild giant pandas.

SCHALLER, GEORGE B., HU JINCHU, PAN WENSHI, and ZHU JING. *The Giant Pandas of Wolong.* Chicago: The University of Chicago Press, 1985. A detailed and authoritative account of the giant panda's habits and requirements in the wild, based on the authors' research in the Wolong Reserve in Sichuan.

Schaller has also written a number of articles about his experiences and his panda research. Among these are two which appeared in the *National Geographic Magazine:* "Pandas in the Wild." December, 1981 (Vol.

160, No. 6), pp. 735–749; and "Secrets of the Wild Giant Panda." March, 1986 (Vol. 169, No. 3), pp. 284–309. *Animal Kingdom*, the publication of the New York Zoological Society, published his article, "Zhen-Zhen, Rare Treasure of Sichuan" in its December, 1982–January, 1983 issue (Vol. 85, No. 6), pp. 5–14; and "Notes of a Professional Panda-Watcher" in its July–August, 1987 issue (Vol. 90, No. 4), pp. 20–25.

*SCHLEIN, MIRIAM. *Project Panda Watch*. New York: Atheneum, 1984. Good account for young readers of panda natural history and research.

SHELDON, WILLIAM. *The Wilderness Home of the Giant Panda*. Amherst: University of Massachusetts Press, 1975. A detailed and very interesting account of a collecting trip in China's Sichuan Province in 1934, sponsored by the American Museum of Natural History. The author was a member of the expedition.

XIN JIGUANG (Editor). *The Giant Panda*. Beijing: China Pictorial, 1984. Many outstanding color photographs of giant pandas, both in the wild and in captivity, as well as Sichuan landscapes and native plants and animals. Supplemented with a short text in English by Wang Zongyi.